IF YOU WERE A

RABBIT

by Carol Watson · pictures by Frances Cony

Published by Dinosaur Publications

If you were a rabbit you would want to run and hop about and dig in the earth.

You would like to nibble grass and leaves and be with other rabbits.

Imagine how you would feel if a large person shut you up in a tiny hutch all day long.

Think how lonely and frightened you would be if dogs and cats came to stare in at you.

The best home for a tame rabbit is a hutch which opens out onto a garden.

This must have a secure fence or wall around it so the rabbit is safe from other animals and cannot run away.

Rabbits burrow deep underground, so the fence or wall will need to be sunk into the ground.

A rabbit does not like to be cramped.

Its hutch should be large so it can move around easily.

There should be a large wire mesh door so the rabbit can see out.

Like you, a rabbit needs somewhere warm and cosy to sleep. The hutch should have two rooms so that the rabbit can hide away from the cold winds.

Make sure the sleeping compartment has lots of hay to make a nest in and a wooden door for privacy.

Try to keep your rabbit's
home high up off the ground.
This will keep it safe from
dogs and cats and stop it
getting damp.

Do not put the hutch anywhere that is too windy or sunny. If the weather is hot, move it to the shade.

If it is very cold, try to bring it indoors.

Like you, a rabbit needs to have friends.
It is much kinder to keep two or three rabbits
than just one on its own. Female rabbits can
live happily together, sharing a large hutch,
but male rabbits need to live on their own.

If you have only one rabbit, make sure it is not lonely. Spend time with it each day, stroking and talking to it.

Sometimes rabbits can make friends with guinea pigs, and some other animals.

Rabbits need two good meals a day. One of these should be cereal and pellets, the other should be vegetables or fruit.

You can buy a mixture of oats, bran, mixed corn, rabbit pellets and flaked maize.
Try adding some warm water
or milk to make it tasty. Another
kind of mash is wholemeal bread
with hot or cold milk.

Rabbits love fresh vegetables. Favourites are carrots, celery, cabbage, lettuce and spinach. They like apples and pears as well, but not too often.

In the wild, rabbits spend much of their day feeding, and tame rabbits like to nibble all day long too. It is kind to give your rabbit some hay every day, but put it in a rack away from the floor to keep it fresh.

Give your rabbit water in a drip-feed bottle, which you hang on the wall of the hutch. Water in pots often gets dirty or spilled.

It is important to clean out the hutch every day to keep it smelling fresh.

Spread cat litter, wood chippings or peat on the floor of the hutch.
Beware! Do not use newspapers – the print is poisonous.

The sleeping compartment should have a
deep layer of hay to keep your rabbit warm.

Give your rabbit
a bark-covered log
to use as a gnawing block.

If you let your rabbits out during the day,
always make sure you shut them safely
back in the hutch at night.

Rabbits are very good at grooming. If you keep their hutch clean and feed them properly, they will stay healthy and their fur will keep in good condition.

Brush your rabbit as often as you can. It will like the attention and become more friendly. In the summer, rabbits moult, and brushing helps to remove all the loose hairs.

Never lift a rabbit only by its ears or only by the scruff of its neck. Use both hands and cradle it against your body. To put it back in its hutch, lower it in hind legs first, then it cannot kick or scratch you.

Ears are **NOT** handles

Health
Rabbits do sometimes get ailments.

Fleas, lice and nits
If you see your rabbit scratching, it may have these. Check the fur around its neck and head. You can buy special powder from the chemist which kills pests. Clean the hutch thoroughly. Put in fresh hay and litter.

Mites
If your rabbit scratches its ears and shakes its head a lot, it may have ear mites. Take it to the vet.

Claws
Wild rabbits wear their claws down by burrowing, but tame rabbits may need to have them clipped. It is kinder to let the vet do this.

Teeth
Rabbits' front teeth keep growing all through their life. Tame rabbits who do not gnaw enough sometimes have problems.

To keep the teeth healthy, it is important to have a gnawing block and to feed your pet vegetables on the stalk when you can.

Snuffles

If your rabbit sneezes or has a runny
nose, take him to the vet
straight away. When a rabbit catches
a cold it is very serious.

Wounds

Rabbits sometimes fight. If they are
only slightly hurt, bathe the wound
with a mild antiseptic. If serious, take
them to the vet.

Always try to keep a sick rabbit separate from the others.

Tips for rabbit owners

A small or medium-sized rabbit is best choice for a pet.

Make sure your rabbit is healthy when you buy it. Try to get one from a specialist breeder if you can.

A hutch for two small or medium-sized rabbits should be at least 150 × 60 × 60 cm.

The layer of litter on the floor of the hutch should be at least 5cm deep.

If you are making an enclosure to exercise your rabbit, the fencing will need to be at least 1 metre high and sunk into the ground to prevent them escaping through burrowing.